The Life and Times of Lilly the Lash

The Garden Gathering
Written By Julie Woik

To Reese -
 Wow!! you are so fantastic. your smile is so bright... It lights up the whole sky.

Isn't that cool?!?

Yahoooooo

Merry Christmas 2009

Advocate House,
an imprint of
A Cappela Publishing, Inc.
P.O. Box 3691
Sarasota, FL 34230-3691

Library of Congress Cataloging in Publication Data
Woik Julie
The Garden Gathering
(Book #1 in The Life and Times of Lilly the Lash series)

p.   cm.
ISBN 978-0-9779139-4-7
1. Fiction, Juvenile   2. Psychology, self-esteem 3. Multi-cultural

First Edition
10 9 8 7 6 5 4 3 2 1

Design: Elsa K. Holderness
Illustration: Marc Tobin

Published by Advocate House, Sarasota, Florida
Printed in the United States of America

DEDICATION

To my husband Finn
I am grateful
for every second,
of every hour,
of every day
that I have known you.
Thank you for loving me.

Your Wife

THE GARDEN GATHERING

Book #1 in the Series
The Life and Times of Lilly the Lash

Early one morning, as the garden awoke,
The daisies sipped coffee while the hummingbird spoke.
Telling a tale that would make them all laugh,
Causing the blue bells to double in half.

The daybreak inspired a fresh start everyday,
　　With dew drops unleashing each flower's bouquet.
Dragonflies and bumble bees, dancing around,
　　Riding the leaves as they'd float to the ground.

Some of these flowers had been here before,
Waking from winter to blossom once more.
Embracing each day, like the very first time,
They broke through the soil to embark on their climb.

Spring was approaching and new seeds would start,
    The process that makes them a true piece of art.
They'd bathe in the sun, giving glow to their cheeks,
    Becoming full grown in a matter of weeks.

While waiting for nature to get in full swing,
A guest had arrived, on Old Shadow Hawk's wing.
Just as they flew past the wall made of stone, Lilly waved

"Thank youuuuu"

and jumped to her home.

A summersault later, she'd land with a crash,
You'd expect nothing less from Ms. Lilly the Lash.
Although upside down she'd still manage a smile,
Displaying the charm that created her style.

You're probably wondering who Lilly could be?

Such an odd looking fairy, to land in a tree.
She once was an eyelash, who lived on my face.
Who guided my soul with her goodness and grace.

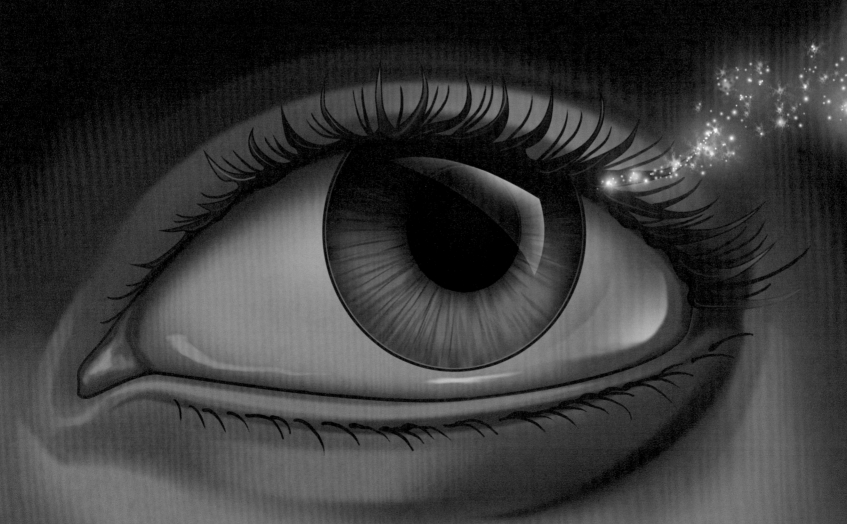

Glistening like stardust you'd find in a dream,
She gave me the strength to build strong self esteem.
Teaching me morals on life and its' flow,
With each of her lessons my spirit would grow.

She often would say to me, "Open your eyes!
If you're not really looking, you'll miss the surprise.
There's more to that flower than just being red...

...See, in the middle, there's a LADYBUG'S BED."

As time carried on it became perfectly clear,
Lilly's purpose was bigger, and she couldn't stay here.
But with her in my thoughts I did not feel alone,
The world was her canvas but my eyelid was home.

So late in the evening,
Lilly gathered her things.
She laced up her shoes
and straightened her wings.

Her butterfly kiss was farewell and good-bye,
Setting off on adventures with a blink of my eye.

Now back to that tree where she's cleared out a spot,

Lilly's lookin' quite cozy in the heart of that knot.
Dragging the twigs from a small vacant nest
To build her a hammock in order to rest.

"Ready, set, go!"

"Ready, set, go!" Lilly called from the sky,
Clapping her hands as she quickly spun by.
Keeping close eye on the garden's good health,
Was the very first mission she'd set for herself.

"An apple a day..."

A young
budding sunflower
appeared on the scene.
Voicing concern
that her stem
was not lean.

Checking the mirror
Sunny found on a wall,
Confirmed her suspicion
that she also was tall.

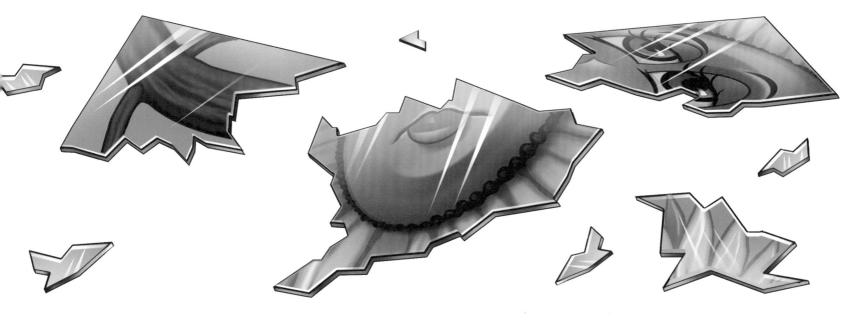

A bit of a stickler, she liked things "just so,"
This image, for Sunny, would be hard to let go.
The thought of her having a big double chin,
Compared to the flowers that grew nice and thin.

When new leaves popped out it drove Sunny insane.
 Of course it was worse if it started to rain.
The additional growth brought on low self esteem,
 And some big, whopping tears that created a stream!

No one but Sunny considered her stance.
They loved what they saw, from the very first glance.
The bright colored petals engulfing her head
Displayed like a crown sewn with fine golden thread.

For all that she was, she could not even see
That the size of her head gave so much to the bees.
And the shade it provided gave Sammy the Snake
A cool, comfy spot for those naps that he'd take.

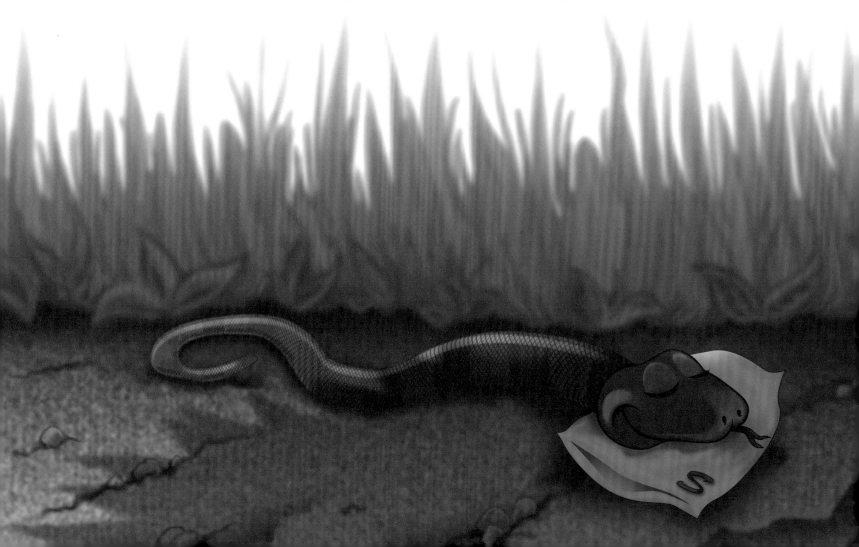

But none of this mattered to Sunny at all.
She could only be great, if she only was small.

It was thinking like this
that caused Lilly concern.
So she drew up a plan
that could help Sunny learn.

The very next night, when the moon fell asleep,
Sunny felt certain she'd heard a faint weep.
Pausing a moment, as to think what to say,
She called to the darkness...

"Can I help in some way?"

A blue speckled spider with dirt on his knees,
Slid down a silk strand that hung high from the trees.

"When I went to play soccer, they left me to last.
And because of my size, they decided to pass."

Arnie hopped onto
the path made of brick.
Collecting his web
three times faster than quick.
Sunny, in awe
at the sight of such speed,
Said...

"Arnie, your moves are extraordinary indeed!"

Grabbing a seat, Arnie tried to explain,
"I'm always too tiny, and feel so ashamed.
To move like the lightning, is no special trait.
If I only was big, then I'd know I'd be great."

Shaking her head,
Sunny couldn't believe,
Arnie down-played
this gift
that could help out
the team.

"You need
to go back there
and show 'em your stuff.

"If it comes from your heart,
they'll catch on soon enough."

Arnie took in the advice Sunny gave,
"You're right!" cried out Arnie, his voice strong and brave.
"Tomorrow I'll move like a rocket in space,
To prove being small doesn't matter in this case."

From behind the wood fence
Lilly watched with delight,
Preparing the satchel
she'd use during the flight.

A place for the magical sprinkles to hide,
While Lilly prepared for her breathtaking ride.

Down came the sparkles, like fresh fallen snow,
To gracefully paint Sunny's eye with a glow.

This sign was exactly what Lilly had planned,
To assure her that Sunny would now understand.

Sunny looked up and cried out to the stars,
    "Why can't we like ourselves, just as we are?"
Sunny now realized how foolish she'd been,
    Not allowing herself that great love from within.

It took a wee spider to make it all clear,
A "sizeable" difference was nothing to fear.
We're all one big puzzle and each of us holds
A piece that tomorrow, will need to unfold.

Lilly would pack up
      her things the next day.
With the job here complete,
      she did not need to stay.
She'd travel around
      seeking souls to repair,
Should you find you're in need,
      close your eyes, she'll be there.

The End

. . . are you sure?

Did you know . . .

FUN FACTS

 Hummingbirds have a wing beat range from 50 to 200 beats per second. They can fly up, down, right, left, backwards, upside down and even loop-de-loops! Amazing!

 Bluebells are fragrant bell-shaped flowers that stand upright when in bud, but hang downward, nodding in the breeze when fully open.

 Dragonflies were around before the dinosaurs! The oldest known dragonfly lived 300 million years ago. The largest known dragonfly had a wingspan of 24 inches.

 The Wag-Tail Dance - A dance performed by a honeybee to tell other honeybees how far away to hunt for new flowers. The direction that the bee dances while moving her tail tells where the flowers are in relation to the sun. It is interesting to note that the number of wags she makes in 15 seconds tells how far away the flowers are!

 Hawks have a pouch called a crop, located halfway between their mouth and stomach. The crop stores food, and gradually releases it to the hawk's stomach, as needed.

 The spots on a ladybug fade as they get older. Ladybugs chew from side to side and not up and down like people do.

 The tallest sunflower grown on record was 25 feet tall, and the largest sunflower head on record measured 32 1/2 inches across its widest point.

 Snakes have 6 rows of teeth, four on top and two on the bottom. They move slower than an adult human can run; the fastest recorded speed achieved by any snake is about 8 mph, but few can go that fast.

 Spiderwebs can get dirty and torn, so most spiders build a new web everyday. What do they do with the old web? Roll it up into a ball and eat it. Yummy!

Lilly's goin' BIG
(The Big Apple that is!)

The Life and Times of Lilly the Lash
The Toy Store

"Whaahooooooooo!" shouted Lilly, as she whizzed down the slide,
Flailing her arms, to the bottom of the ride.
"I finally found the ideal place to land,
The torch that Ms. Liberty holds in her hand!"

A jump to her feet, Lilly checked the brochure,
Tomorrow she'd plan for a city wide tour.
Observing the sights and the sounds for a trace,
Hoping they'd lead her to just the right place.

The night would creep in, changing buildings and cars,
To a dazzling spectrum of diamond-like stars.
This place was alive, with a heart and a soul,
The perfect location for Lilly's next goal.

(Watch for Book #2 in this Series)

Follow Lilly on her next adventure to
New York City
Where a young boy learns the important
Life Lesson of
SHARING

ACKNOWLEDGEMENTS

To the Illustrator
Thank you Marc, for helping me make this dream come true.
Your exuberant personality, "side-splitting" sense of humor, and
superior quality of work was *exactly* what I had been searching for!
And Brigitte…well, she is just the icing on the cake.
You are both truly WONDERFUL people.
(Dozer and Morey are pretty cool too!!)

To the Designer
Elsa…You are a smart, sweet, SPECIAL woman.
I am forever thankful to the spirits (and Gail)
for bringing you into my life.
Thank you for your support and friendship!

To Patrika - A Capella Publishing
Our travels often lead us down windy roads.
Thank you for guiding me through the turns,
and reminding me to breathe.
Onward and upward!

Beyond Thanks
To my Mom and Dad
I have no words to thank you for what you have given to me.
Your tender, caring, moral ways, your stable, secure household,
and never, ever, ending love and support, have provided me with the
necessary tools to live my life with strong self-esteem and respect,
while filling my heart with boundless compassion for others.
Even Lilly couldn't have dreamed up better parents!

To my "CUZ"
Thank you for making me feel *just* like a sister.
(And, by the way, Mom said she always DID like me best
…but not to tell you!)

SPECIAL THANKS

To Ed and Cindy
Your perpetual enthusiasm, encouragement, and love
have fueled this ride from the very beginning.
I am forever indebted to the shooting stars responsible
for dropping the both of you into our lives!
And you…Ms. Cindy…it's all about you!

To Becky
The day I was given the gift of our friendship,
I could in no way have foreseen the multitude of lessons
we were destined to encounter in the days to follow.
Our experiences together have often brought on emotions
I wasn't even aware existed. What an exciting way to live life!
Thank you for your lifetime of friendship,
and extraordinary way of loving me unconditionally.

To Patti
I feel so very fortunate to have your constant
show of support and excitement in all of my endeavors.
Thank you for cheering me on, and loving me even MORE on bad hair days!!
I am a very lucky gal!

To Shari
Thank GOODNESS your children attended that exclusive
Pre-School Ivy League Business College!
Without them, I don't know where I'd be?!
Thanks Ryen, Caitlynne, and Lauren

To Carol
hankfully you knew how to find the right color bow for a polka dotted toad!
You might just be the best cut and paste artist around.
Thanks for the laughs!

To Jason, Irma, Desi, Bob, Pistol Pete…
and the countless other wonderful friends who have so kindly shared
their lives and experiences with me.
You are Priceless!

And to Kim
A boss 8-5…my friend 24/7.
I've laughed so much with you, "my insides are all wrung"!!!

Making Our World

A Better Place

A percentage of the profit from
this book will go to the:
**H. Lee Moffitt Cancer Center &
Research Institute, Specifying: Research**

To my very special friend
Irene Fernandez

As of today, I have yet to meet you.
Your gallant spirit, uplifting attitude, and fearless inner strength
have given me ENDLESS inspiration.
You are absolutely remarkable beyond belief!
Thank you for sharing your amazing journey with me.
I love you with all my heart Irene, Julie